GOOD MORNING, SNOWPLOW!

BY DEBORAH BRUSS

ART BY LOU FANCHER AND STEVE JOHNSON

Arthur A. Levine Books An Imprint of Scholastic Inc.

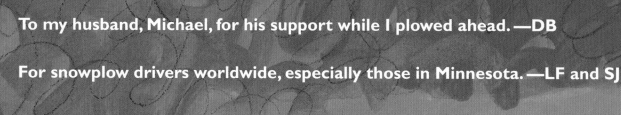

To my husband, Michael, for his support while I plowed ahead. —DB

For snowplow drivers worldwide, especially those in Minnesota. —LF and SJ

Text copyright © 2018 by Deborah Bruss
Art copyright © 2018 by Johnson and Fancher, Inc.

All rights reserved. Published by Arthur A. Levine Books,
an imprint of Scholastic Inc., *Publishers since 1920.*
SCHOLASTIC and the LANTERN LOGO are trademarks
and/or registered trademarks of Scholastic Inc.

The publisher does not have any control over and does not assume
any responsibility for author or third-party websites or their content.

No part of this publication may be reproduced, stored in a retrieval system, or transmitted in any form
or by any means, electronic, mechanical, photocopying, recording, or otherwise, without written permission
of the publisher. For information regarding permission, write to Scholastic Inc., Attention: Permissions
Department, 557 Broadway, New York, NY 10012.

This book is a work of fiction. Names, characters, places, and incidents are either the product
of the author's imagination or are used fictitiously, and any resemblance to actual persons,
living or dead, business establishments, events, or locales is entirely coincidental.

Library of Congress Cataloging-in-Publication Data available

ISBN 978-1-338-08949-3

10 9 8 7 6 5 4 3 2 1   18 19 20 21 22

Printed in China 62
First edition, November 2018

The text type was set in 14-point Gill Sans MT Bold.
The display type was set in Rosemary Regular.
The art for this book was created using
acrylic paint, colored pencil, pen, and collage.
Art direction and book design by Marijka Kostiw

Good night, homes, and good night, cars.

Clouds move in to hide the stars.

Good night, farms, and good night, town.

Tiny flakes start twirling down.

Good night, playground turning white.

Good night, snowplow? Not tonight!

Start the engine. Try the lights.

Check both signals — left, then right.

Fill the hopper. Test the brakes.

Driver's ready? Wide awake!

Chains are down. Time to go.

Roads will soon be blocked with snow.

Drop the plow, extend the wing.

Giant drifts won't melt till spring.

Strobe on top sweeps round and round.

Frosted branches touch the ground.

Waves of white curl off the blade.

In its wake, a trail is laid.

How's the road? A little slick?

Salt and sand mix does the trick.

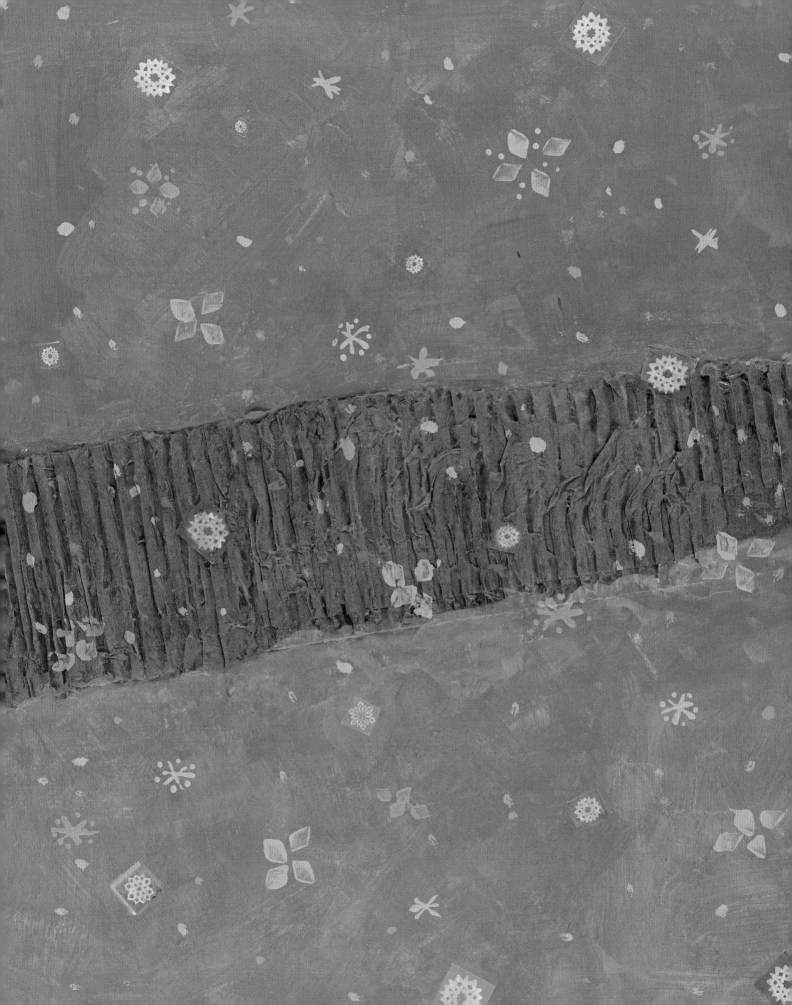

Lonely plowing all night long.

Tune the dial and sing a song.

Windshield wipers keeping time.

Washers squirt to clear the grime.

Car approaches much too fast.

Slipping, sliding, zips on past.

Digging out will be tough going.

Call the dispatch. Car needs towing.

Wind picks up and whirls the snow.

It's a whiteout! Take it slow.

Watch the flags and feel the road.

Push on with your heavy load.

Snow keeps falling fast and deep.

Miles to plow before you sleep.

Pay attention. What's ahead?

Take no chances. Stop instead.

Step outside and look around.

All is hushed . . . not a sound.

Clean the lights in front and back.

Hear what's coming down the track.

Front light leading, barely glowing.

Engine chugging, but not slowing.

Cloud of white grows as it nears.

Train blows by and disappears.

Scrape and salt and sand all night.

Soon the sky is streaked with light.

Wake up, farms! Wake up, town!

No more snowflakes swirling down.

School is canceled. Playground covered.

Bright new day to be discovered.

Roads no longer buried deep.

Good morning, snowplow . . .

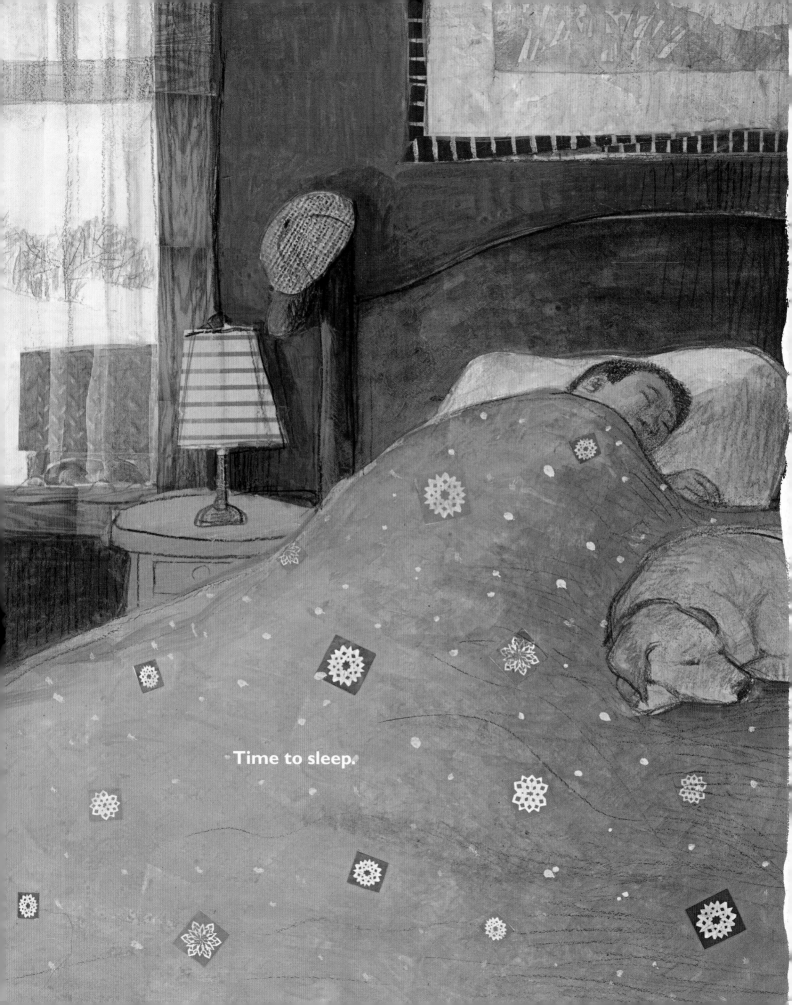

Time to sleep.